HANS CHRISTIAN ANDERSEN'S
FAIRY TALES

THE CLASSIC CHILDREN'S TREASURY

Hans Christian
Andersen's
Fairy Tales

The Classic Children's Treasury

Retold by William King

With Illustrations by

Leon Baxter · Joan Martin May

Graham Percy · Gary Rees

Kay Widdowson · Jenny Williams

Courage
BOOKS

AN IMPRINT OF RUNNING PRESS
PHILADELPHIA · LONDON

9 8 7 6 5 4 3 2 1
Digit on the right indicates the number of this printing

ISBN 1-56138-765-7
Library of Congress Cataloging-in-Publication Number
96-67219

Cover illustration by Graham Percy
Illustrations by Leon Baxter, Joan Martin May,
Graham Percy, Gary Rees, Kay Widdowson, and Jenny Williams
Cover and interior design by Ian Butterworth
Edited by Elaine M. Bucher

Published by Courage Books, an imprint of
Running Press Book Publishers
125 South Twenty-second Street
Philadelphia, Pennsylvania 19103-4399

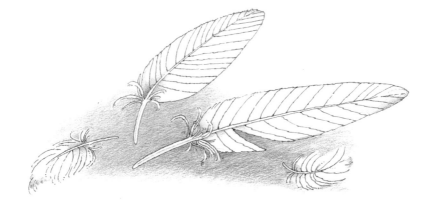

INTRODUCTION

Hans Christian Andersen led a life that was something of a fairy tale.

Born into a poor family in Denmark in 1805, Andersen received little formal schooling until his late teens, when a benefactor enrolled him in a private school. Soon after this, he began to write. He wrote his first children's tale in 1835, and went on to compose more than 150 of these exquisite stories during his lifetime.

The stories in this book are selected from Andersen's most imaginative and best-known works, and they invite us into a world filled with magic, love, and bravery.

CONTENTS

The Emperor's New Clothes

Many years ago there lived an emperor who was so fond of fine clothes that he spent all his money on new robes and other royal attire. He didn't care about his soldiers, or the theater, nor visiting the park, except when he wanted to show off his new outfits. He owned an outfit for every hour of the day!

One day two wanderers came to the city. They called themselves weavers, and said they knew how to weave the most splendid cloth anyone could imagine. Not only were the colors and the patterns grand, but the clothes were made so that they were invisible to anyone who was stupid.

"They must be fine clothes indeed!" thought the emperor when he heard of these weavers. *"I must have that cloth made for me at once."* And so he gave the two wanderers many gold pieces and a room in the castle so that they could begin their work at once.

The two wanderers set up two looms and pretended to work, but they really had nothing on their looms. They ordered the finest silk and the costliest gold. This they put in their own bags, and worked away at the empty looms until late at night.

"I'd like to know how much of the cloth they have ready now," thought the emperor a week later, but he felt uneasy at the idea that whoever was stupid could not see the cloth.

He thought, of course, that *he* would be able to see the cloth, but first he wanted someone to see how the weavers were progressing.

"I will send my old, honest advisor to the weavers," thought the emperor. *"He can see what the cloth looks like."*

So the old and trusty advisor went into the room where the two wanderers sat working at the empty looms. *"Dear me!"* thought the old advisor, and opened his eyes wide. *"I don't see anything!"*

The two wanderers asked him to come nearer, and asked him how he liked the fine pattern and the beautiful colors. They pointed to the empty looms, and the poor advisor opened his eyes even wider, but he still couldn't see anything, because there was nothing to see.

"Oh my!" he thought. *"Am I really so stupid? It would never do to say that I can't see the cloth."*

"Well, how do you like it?" asked one of the weavers.

"Oh, it is really fine," said the old advisor. "What a pattern, and what colors! I shall tell the emperor that I am very much pleased with it."

"We are happy to hear that," said the weavers. They then spoke about the colors by their names, and talked about the wonderful pattern. The old advisor listened to them very closely so that he could repeat what they said when he returned to the emperor, and this he did.

The weavers now asked for more money, more silk, and more gold, which they said they needed to complete their work. Once again, they put everything they received from the emperor in their own bags. Then they kept on weaving at the empty looms.

The emperor soon sent another trusted counselor to see how the weaving went. Again the emperor's counselor looked and looked, but there was nothing to see except the empty looms.

"Isn't this a fine piece of cloth?" asked the two weavers. They pretended to show off the cloth.

"I'm not stupid," thought the counselor, *"but I don't see anything! Whatever I do, I can't let anyone know."*

So the counselor praised the cloth, which he did not see, and expressed his

delight at the beautiful colors and the splendid pattern.

"Yes, it is a marvel," he later told the emperor.

All the people in the town were soon talking about the splendid cloth. At last the emperor wished to see it himself. With a whole company of chosen men, including the two trusted advisors who had been there before, he visited the two cunning wanderers.

They were working away with all their might, without any thread or material whatsoever.

"Isn't it magnificent?" asked the two weavers. "What does your majesty think of the pattern and the colors?" Then they pointed to the empty looms.

"How can this be?" thought the emperor. *"I see nothing. Am I stupid? Am I not fit to be emperor? This is really dreadful."*

Finally the emperor said, "Yes, this is very fine." He nodded approvingly at the empty looms. He wouldn't say that *he* couldn't see anything.

None of his advisors could see anything, either. Just like the emperor, however, they said, "It is very fine," and they advised him to have the weavers use the new cloth to make clothes for the emperor to wear at the great procession which was to take place soon.

The night before the procession was to take place, the weavers were up all night getting everything ready until they said at last, "The clothes are ready."

The emperor, with his most distinguished courtiers, came to the weavers' room. One of the weavers lifted his arms as if he were holding something and said, "See, here are the trousers, here is the coat, and here is the cloak," and so on.

"It's as light as a cobweb," the weavers said. "You would think you had nothing on at all, but that's just the beauty of it."

"Yes," said all the courtiers, but they didn't see anything, because there was nothing to see.

"Will your majesty please take off your clothes?" said the weavers. "We will put the new clothes on your majesty."

The emperor took off his clothes, and the weavers pretended to give him the new clothes, piece by piece. When the weavers said they were done, the emperor turned around in all directions before a large mirror.

"How splendidly they fit!" they all said. "What a pattern! What colors!"

"They are waiting outside with the canopy which is to be held over your majesty in the procession," said the leader of the ceremonies.

"I am quite ready," said the emperor. And he turned around once more before the mirror, to make everyone believe that he was really admiring his new clothes.

And so the emperor went in the procession under a splendid canopy. All the people in the streets said, "What handsome new clothes the emperor has! How beautifully they fit him!" Nobody would admit they saw nothing, because they were afraid to appear stupid.

"But he hasn't got anything on!" cried a child.

"Just listen to what the little innocent says!" said the boy's mother. Soon the people whispered to each other what the child had said.

"He hasn't got anything on!" shouted the people at last.

This made the emperor anxious, since he knew they were right. But the emperor thought, *"I must keep up appearances through the procession."*

And the emperor walked on still more majestically, and his aides walked behind and carried his imaginary train, which didn't exist at all.

SILLY HANS

Out in the country there was an old mansion, and in it lived an old squire and two of his sons, Peter and Stephen. Both sons wanted to woo the king's daughter, who had announced that she would marry the man who could best speak for himself.

Peter and Stephen took two weeks to prepare themselves. Peter used a dictionary to learn hundreds of new words. Stephen practiced speaking and gesturing in front of a mirror.

"I shall win the princess," said both of them. Their father gave each of them a beautiful horse. The brothers dressed in their fanciest clothes in hopes of impressing the princess.

Just as Peter and Stephen were mounting their horses to ride to the castle, their brother rode up. Now, no one paid very much attention to this third brother. He liked to travel around the countryside, and he was known as Silly Hans.

"Where are you two going, all dressed up?" asked Hans.

"To the palace, to woo the king's daughter," they replied. "Haven't you heard?"

"No. But I'll come, too!" said Hans. But his brothers rode away without him.

"Father, let me have a horse," pleaded Hans. "I want to ask the princess to marry me." But his father thought Hans was too foolish for the princess, and he wouldn't give Hans a horse. So Hans went out into the barn, found a billy goat, hopped on, and soon was on his way.

"Hello!" shouted Hans when he caught up to his brothers. "Look what I found in the road: a dead crow!"

"Foolish boy, what are you going to do with that?" they asked.

"I'll make a present of it for the king's daughter," said Hans. His brothers laughed at him and rode on.

"Brothers!" shouted Hans a little later. "Look what I found now: an old wooden shoe."

"Will you give *that* to the princess as well?" asked Stephen.

"Yes," replied Hans. Shaking their heads in wonderment, his brothers continued on ahead.

After a bit, the two brothers heard Hans again calling their names. When they turned around, they saw Hans riding toward them holding a large handful of mud.

"Ugh," said Peter and Stephen together. "Don't tell us that you intend to give that to the princess."

"Certainly," answered Hans. "This is some of the finest mud, and the princess deserves the very best."

"Enough of this foolishness," said Peter and Stephen, and they raced off.

Peter and Stephen soon joined a long line of suitors who sought the princess's hand in marriage. As each suitor entered the room where the princess sat, however, each one seemed to lose the power of speech.

"Away with you," said the princess as a suitor stood silently before her.

At last, it was Peter's turn. But as soon as Peter saw the princess, he forgot all the words he had learned and couldn't think of anything to say. Finally he mumbled, "It's very hot in here."

"Yes, that's because I'm roasting chickens today," said the princess jokingly.

Peter was at a complete loss for words. He hadn't expected such a reply from the princess, so he stood dumbfounded, unable to reply.

"Enough," said the princess after a moment, and Peter left.

Stephen entered next, but he did just as badly as his brother, and the princess sent him away.

Suddenly there was a commotion at the door, and in rode Hans on his billy goat!

"Hello princess!" said Hans. "How hot it is in here."

"That's because I'm roasting chickens today," replied the princess, expecting Hans to falter.

"That's fine," replied Hans. "Can I get a crow roasted here?" And he took the dead crow out of his pocket.

"That you may," said the princess, "but you'll need something to roast it in, for I have neither pot nor pan."

"I do," said Hans, and with that he took out the old wooden shoe he had found and put the crow in it.

"That's enough for a meal," said the princess, "but what will you flavor the crow with?"

"I have the seasoning in my pocket," said Hans. Hans then put some of the mud on the crow.

"That's what I like," said the princess. "You think on your feet, and you have a sense of humor. You will be my husband."

And so Hans married the princess, and eventually he was made king. He became a just and fair king, and the people of the kingdom loved him and the queen, and they all lived happily ever after.

THE STEADFAST TOY SOLDIER

There were once twenty-five tin soldiers who were all brothers, since they were all born from the same old tin spoon. They all shouldered their muskets, they all looked straight ahead, and they all wore the same splendid red-and-blue uniform.

The first words they heard in this world, when the lid was taken off the box in which they lived, were: "Toy soldiers!"

It was a little boy who shouted this as he clapped his hands in delight at seeing the soldiers.

The tin soldiers were all exactly alike, except one, and he had only one leg because he had been made last of all, and there wasn't enough tin to fill the mold. But he stood just as firm on his one leg as the others on their two.

On the table where all the tin soldiers had been placed stood many other toys, but the most remarkable of all was a splendid castle made of cardboard. In front of the castle were some small trees. Swans made of wax swam on a mirror that served as a lake.

It was all very pretty, but the prettiest of all was a little doll who stood right outside the open gate of the castle.

She was cut out of paper, but she had a skirt of pure silk, and a little narrow blue ribbon over her shoulders, just like a scarf, and in the middle of it was a bright spangle as big as her face. The doll stretched out both her arms—she was a dancer—and she lifted one leg so high that the tin soldier couldn't see it, and he believed that she had only one leg like himself.

"That's the wife for me," he thought; *"but she's very grand: she lives in a castle. I have only a box, and there are twenty-five of us there already. I must try and get acquainted with her."* He then crouched down behind a box on the table. There he could have a good look at the beautiful dancer, who remained standing on one leg without losing her balance.

Later on in the evening all the other tin soldiers were put back in their box, and the people in the house went to bed. Then the toys commenced to play. The nutcracker turned somersaults, and the pencil did tricks on the paper.

The only two who didn't stir from their places were the tin soldier and the little dancer. He never took his eyes off her for a moment. The clock struck twelve and suddenly—BOUNCE!—the lid flew off the box in front of the toy soldier. It was a jack-in-the-box!

"Tin soldier," shouted the jack, "keep your eyes to yourself!" When the tin soldier didn't answer, the jack said, "Just you wait until tomorrow!"

When morning came and the children were up, the tin soldier was put in the window, and whether it was a sudden breeze or the jack's words, the window flew open and the soldier fell headfirst out of the window.

He fell to the ground and wound up standing on his head, with his bayonet sticking between two stones in the pavement. The servant girl and the little boy ran down to the street to look for the soldier, but they couldn't seem to find him. Soon it began to rain and the two children went back in the house.

When the rain was over, two boys walked by and said, "Look! There's a soldier. Let's give him a sail." The boys made a little boat out of newspaper, and soon the soldier was sailing along the gutter.

The paper boat rocked up and down, and now and then it turned about so rapidly that the soldier was nearly shaken overboard, but the soldier hung on.

All of a sudden the boat drifted into a drain, where it was very dark. *"I wonder where I'm off to now?"* thought the soldier. *"If only the little dancer were with me, I wouldn't mind if it were twice as dark."*

Just then a large rat, who lived in the drain, saw him. "Do you have a pass?" squeaked the rat. The soldier didn't answer and grasped his musket tightly. The

boat drifted onward. The rat chased after the soldier, gnashing his teeth, but the brave soldier managed to stay in the boat as it began drifting faster and faster until, with one last snap of his jaws, the rat gave up the chase.

Then the tin soldier saw bright daylight at the end of the drain and heard the roaring of a waterfall. Knowing that he couldn't stop the boat, the brave soldier summoned up all his courage and held himself steady. Somehow he made it over the waterfall, but his little boat began to fall apart. Water came in from all sides and soon reached the soldier's head.

Just when the boat went to pieces and the soldier began sinking to the bottom, a fish came along and swallowed the soldier! At first the soldier was frightened, because it was even darker inside the fish than in the drain. But the soldier was brave, and he didn't flinch. The fish, though, wiggled wildly until suddenly it became still. For a while everything was dark and silent.

Then there was a flash of lightning and the soldier heard a voice say, "It's a toy soldier!"

The fish had been caught and taken to market, where it was sold. A cook had bought the fish and cut it open, only to discover the soldier.

The cook picked up the soldier and took him into the living room to show everyone the amazing soldier that had traveled inside the fish. The cook put him on a table, and what did the soldier see but the castle and all of the other toys. He was in the same house he had left!

The soldier saw that all of the toys were there, including the little dancer. *"Has she been waiting for me?"* thought the soldier. He looked at her and she looked at him, but they didn't say anything.

Right then one of the little boys picked up the soldier and threw him into the lit fireplace, without giving any reason for doing so; it must have been the jack from the jack-in-the-box who put the thought into his head.

The heat in the fireplace was terrible, but all the toy soldier could think of was the little dancer. Soon he began to melt, but he tried to stand firm while he and the dancer looked at one another.

Suddenly one of the doors in the room flew open, and the draft caught the dancer and blew her into the fireplace, right next to the tin soldier! There was a blaze of flames, and then no one could see either of the toys.

The next day, though, when the servants shook out the ashes, they found that the tin soldier had melted down into a little tin heart. And all that was left of the dancer was her spangle, which was burned as black as coal.

The Princess And The Pea

Once upon a time there was a prince who wanted to marry a princess, but only a *true* princess. So he traveled all over the world to find one.

He met many princesses, but there was something about each one that made him wonder whether she was a true princess. After searching far and wide for many years, he returned home quite distressed, for he wanted very much to find a true princess.

One evening a terrible storm set in. There was lightning and thunder, and the rain poured down in torrents. All at once there was a knock at the gate of the palace, and the old king went to the gate.

Outside stood a pretty young woman. And what a sight she was! The water ran down her hair and clothes, and into her shoes. She said that she was a princess who had escaped from bandits on the road to the castle.

"We shall soon find out if you are a true princess," thought the king to himself as he led her into the palace. But he said nothing. A few minutes later, while servants built a roaring fire in the fireplace so that the princess could warm herself, the king went into a guest bedroom, took off all the sheets, and put a fresh green pea in the middle of the bed. He then took twenty mattresses and put them on top of the pea, and then he put twenty goosefeather pillows on top of the mattresses.

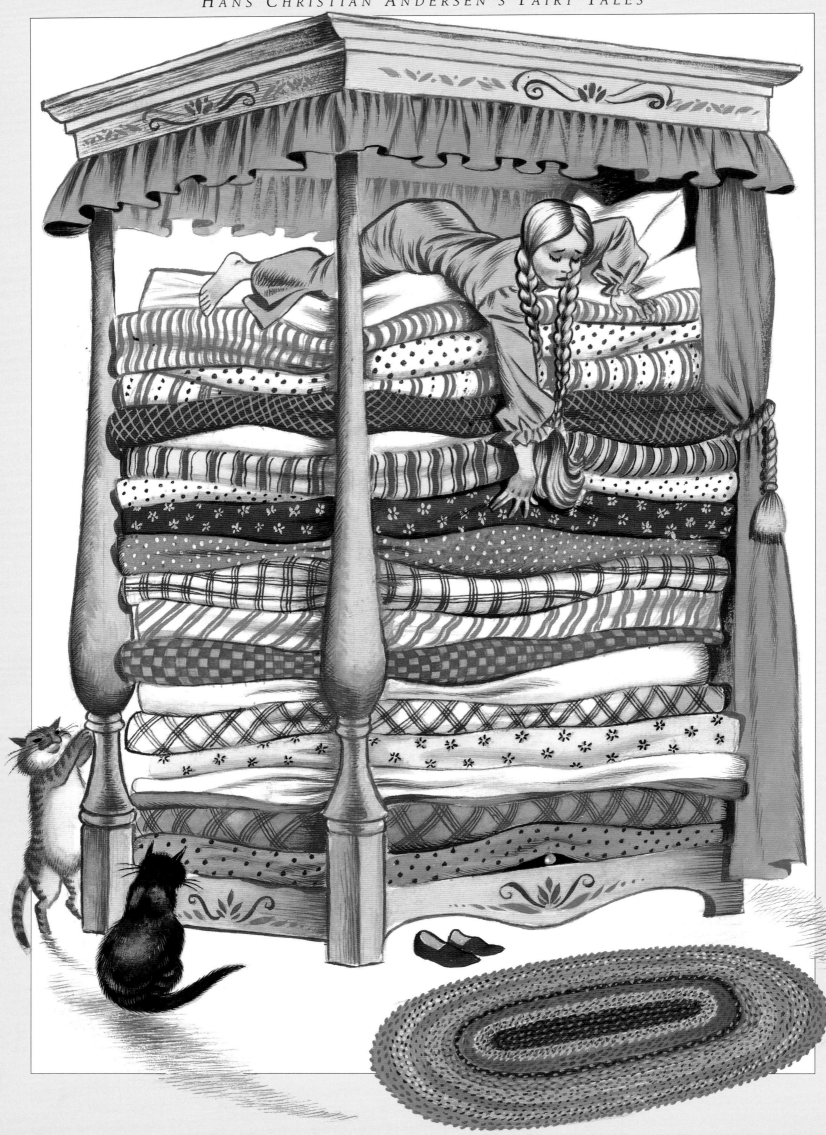

There the princess was to sleep that night.

In the morning, the king asked the princess how she had slept.

"Oh, horribly!" said the princess. "I hardly closed my eyes the whole night. Goodness knows what was in the bed. I have been lying on something hard until I am black and blue all over. It was really terrible!"

Then the king knew that she was indeed a real princess, since she had felt the pea through twenty mattresses and twenty goosefeather pillows. No one but a real princess could be so tender and delicate.

The prince began to court her, and soon they were married. The pea was placed in the royal museum, where it remains to this day.

THE FIR TREE

Once there stood a very pretty fir tree. It had plenty of space, and sunshine bathed it daily. The forest around it bustled with life, and many other trees grew around it.

This fir tree was in a hurry to grow. It never thought of all the space it had, or the other trees nearby, or the children who sometimes roamed through the forest. The fir tree didn't appreciate any of this. The only thing it thought about was growing larger.

In a year the tree was a bit larger, but still it thought only about being as big as the other trees. It took no pleasure in the sunshine, or the birds, or the clouds.

At Christmas the woodcutters always came and cut down some of the biggest trees.

"*Where are they going?*" wondered the tree as the cut trees were dragged away on wagons.

Many days later, the tree had a chance to ask two sparrows.

"They stand in the greatest glory and splendor that you can imagine," replied the sparrows. "They are placed in the middle of bright rooms and decorated with the most beautiful things. We looked in at the windows and saw them."

"And then what happened?" asked the fir tree.

"That's all we saw," replied the sparrows.

"If only I were tall enough for the tree-cutters to pick me," cried the fir tree. "Maybe they will pick me next Christmas. But next year is so far away!"

"Enjoy the fresh air, your youth, and everything that is beautiful in the forest," replied the sparrows.

But the fir tree could think only of the marvelous scenes that the sparrows had described. All through the next year, all the tree thought about was being chosen for the Christmas celebration. This longing made the tree neglect the natural wonders all around even more.

Finally Christmas arrived again, and the tree-cutters came. The fir tree was now quite large, and it was one of the first to be cut. Soon it was being taken toward town on a wagon. But the tree felt no happiness. It felt only pain when it was cut, and sadness when it was taken away from the forest it knew.

Soon the tree was unloaded into a yard, and two grandly dressed servants placed the tree in the center of a large, elegant room. Then the servants decorated the tree.

They placed white candles on many of the tree's branches, as well as Christmas balls and other pretty decorations. Then they placed stacks of colorful packages underneath the tree.

"I wish it were evening and all of my candles were lighted," thought the tree. *"Will the sparrows fly past the windows and see me? I wonder if I will grow here and remain decorated through the whole year?"*

Evening soon came, and all of the tree's candles were lighted. Before the tree could take in the beauty of the scene, one of the candles set fire to one of the tree's branches and singed it badly.

Luckily, one of the servants quickly put out the fire, but the tree was very anxious.

Soon a crowd of children and adults rushed into the room and gathered around the tree.

After admiring the tree for a moment, the children dashed underneath the tree

to examine the presents. Some of the tree's branches were pushed and pulled by the children as they reached for the finely wrapped presents.

Soon everything was unwrapped and the children were running around the room, showing each other their new toys. Then the children and the adults began to leave, until only a servant remained, and he too left after putting out all of the candles.

"Even though I didn't understand all that happened, everything was so exciting! I can't wait until tomorrow night," thought the tree.

But the next day the servants came and took all of the decorations off the tree and put it in a dark closet.

Here the tree spent many days and nights, thinking about the days in the forest, where there was plenty of fresh air and bright sunshine.

One day the tree heard a "squeak, squeak" and saw a tiny mouse.

"Hello, old fir tree," said the mouse. "Where do you come from?"

"I lived in the forest, where the sun shines and there is fresh air and everything is green and alive," replied the tree. "But I came here for Christmas. The people of the house decorated me beautifully with candles and Christmas balls."

"How happy you must have been, old fir tree," said the mouse.

"I'm not at all old," replied the tree. "I'm in the prime of my life."

"Well, what are you doing cooped up in here, then?" asked the mouse.

The tree was unable to answer the mouse's question. Finally the mouse went away, and the tree thought, *"I can't wait until I am brought out again."*

However, for quite a while no one came. Finally one morning, two servants opened the closet and took the tree out into the yard.

"At last I can enjoy the fresh air, the bright sunshine, and the beautiful birds!" thought the tree.

But then the tree looked at the splendor and freshness of the flowers in the garden and then at its own branches, which were now withered and yellow from the long time in the closet. The tree thought of its bright days in the forest long ago and finally appreciated the life it had once had.

"It's all over!" thought the poor tree. *"If only I had enjoyed myself when I had the chance."*

Just then a servant came and chopped the tree into small pieces. Later, when the pieces of the tree were burned in the fireplace, they made a "pop! pop!" sound. Each "pop!" was a deep sigh from the tree, which was thinking back to a summer day in the forest or a cool winter night under the stars.

And so the tree was burned to ashes and met its end, just as this story has come to its end, as all stories do.

IT'S TRUE!

Once there was a white hen who laid eggs regularly. She was a respectable hen in every way. As she settled down on her perch she pecked herself with her beak, and a little feather fell from her wing.

"There it goes!" she said. "The more I peck myself, the prettier I become." She said this in fun, for she was a happy, respectable hen. And then she took a nap.

All of the hens sat side by side on the perch. The hen who sat next to the white hen was not asleep. She couldn't help telling her neighbor, "Did you hear what was just said? I won't mention names, but there is a hen here who wants to pluck out all of her feathers in order to look fine. She should be ashamed of herself."

Just above these hens sat an owl. Owls have sharp ears, and this owl heard every word which the hen below had said. The owl fanned herself with her wing and said, "I can't believe what I just heard. One of the hens is so vain that she sits plucking out all of her feathers so that everyone will look at her. I must tell my neighbor!" said the owl as she flew off.

"Have you heard the news? Hooh! Hooh!" said the owl to her neighbor. "There is a hen who has plucked out all her feathers to get attention. She will freeze to death, if she is not dead already."

"Where? Where?" asked the neighbor owl.

"In the house opposite," said the first owl. "I have as good as seen it myself. It's almost too improper a story to tell, but it's true. Hooh! Oohooh!"

The owls were so loud that they could be heard by pigeons on top of the house across the way.

"We believe it! We believe every word of it!" cooed the pigeons to one another.

Soon one of the pigeons told the story to the poultry in the yard: "There is a hen—some say there are two—who have plucked out all of their feathers to attract attention. It's a dangerous thing to do; one can catch a cold and die of fever, and they are both dead!"

"Wake up! Wake up!" crowed the cock when he overheard the tale. He began crowing, "There are three hens who have died of a broken heart. They were all in love with a cock, and have plucked out all their feathers. It's a terrible story! I don't want to keep it to myself. Pass it on!"

And so the story went from poultry-yard to poultry-yard, from animal to animal, and at last it came back to the place where it had started.

"There are five hens," so the story ran, "who have plucked out all of their feathers to prove which one was the plumpest. But they started pecking one another until they all bled to death!"

The hen who had lost the loose little feather did not, of course, recognize her own story. Being a respectable hen, she said, "I have the greatest contempt for those hens. But there are many more of that sort. Such things must not be hushed up, and I will do my best to get the story in the papers, so that it will be known all over the country."

Soon a newspaper heard the story and the story appeared in print, so people thought that it must be true! And that's how a little feather became a big story.

THUMBELINA

There once was a woman who wanted very much to have a child. So she went to an old witch who gave her a seed and said, "Here is a seed, but it isn't one that grows in farmers' fields. Put it into a flowerpot and then you'll see!"

The woman raced home and planted the seed, and right then a large, beautiful flower grew up.

"What a beautiful flower," said the woman, and she kissed its lovely petals. Just as she kissed the flower, it opened its petals to reveal a tiny, delicate girl! She was hardly the size of your thumb, so she was called Thumbelina.

The woman loved Thumbelina and made her a bed from a walnut shell, with violet's leaves for sheets and a rose leaf for a comforter.

One night, as Thumbelina lay sleeping in her pretty bed, an ugly toad jumped into the room and saw Thumbelina sleeping.

"She would make a beautiful wife for my son!" said the toad. He took the walnut shell in which Thumbelina slept and jumped into the garden with her.

"Croak, croak!" was all the toad's son could say when he saw the sleeping figure of the girl.

"Sssh!" said the father toad. "If she wakes up, she'll run away. I'll put her on a lily pad in the stream so that she won't run away while we make plans for your wedding."

Out in the stream grew many water lilies. The toad hopped from leaf to leaf until he reached the largest one, in the middle of the stream. Here the toad gently placed Thumbelina.

The next morning, after Thumbelina awoke, she sat sadly in silence, for there was no way she could get ashore.

Later that day, the two toads hopped out to the leaf. The father toad bowed before her and said, "Here is my son. He will be your husband as soon as all of the preparations are ready."

"Croak, croak!" was all the toad's son could say. With this, both toads left. Thumbelina began to cry.

It so happened that just then a school of fish was passing by. They had heard the toads and had seen poor Thumbelina. They felt sorry for her and decided that they had to help. So they chewed through the stalk of the water lily, and soon Thumbelina was sailing down the stream on the lily pad.

Thumbelina sailed past many strange places until the lily pad came to rest at the edge of a cornfield. Thumbelina stepped off the lily pad and began to walk across the cornfield.

She struggled through the cornfield until she came to the door of a field mouse. Thumbelina knocked gently on the door and asked if the mouse could offer her anything to eat.

After seeing the beautiful Thumbelina and hearing her plea, the field mouse opened the door and took her inside. The field mouse fed Thumbelina a good meal and said, "You can stay with me as long as you like if you'll help me clean my house and tell me stories." Thumbelina agreed.

A few days later the field mouse said, "We'll soon have a visitor. My neighbor the mole visits me once a week. He's very rich, and he would make a good husband for you."

Thumbelina didn't care for this type of talk. However, as soon as the mole heard her beautiful voice, he fell in love with her. He was a cautious mole, so he said nothing of his feelings.

When the mole visited again, he asked if Thumbelina and the field mouse would like to take a walk with him through the tunnels. He cautioned them that there was a dead bird in the passageway. The bird apparently had fallen into one of the tunnels.

So off Thumbelina went with the field mouse and the mole. They soon came to the bird, which lay with its wings firmly pressed to its sides and its legs and head drawn up under its feathers.

Thumbelina felt very sad when she saw the bird, which was a swallow. The mole and the field mouse continued on their walk, but Thumbelina stayed and tried to cover the dead swallow with some pieces of hay.

When she bent over the swallow, however, she felt the beating of its heart. It was alive!

Thumbelina fed the swallow some pieces of bread that she carried in her pocket, and soon the swallow opened its eyes.

"Many thanks," said the swallow finally. "I fell asleep one cold night, and somehow I came here. I must finish my trip. Would you like to come with me?"

Thumbelina wanted very much to leave, but she knew that the field mouse would be very sad if she left suddenly.

"No, I can't leave," said Thumbelina finally.

"Farewell then," replied the swallow. "I'll always remember your kindness." With that, the swallow burst through the roof of the passageway and flew away.

Thumbelina ran to catch up with the field mouse and the mole. When she told

them what had happened, the mole said, "Bah! Swallows are useless animals! All day it's 'Tweet, tweet! Tweet, tweet!' And this one ruined my passageway. Humph!"

A few days later, the mole came to the field mouse's house and asked to see Thumbelina. When she appeared, the mole asked for her hand in marriage.

The field mouse saw that Thumbelina was very upset and whispered, "Don't be stubborn, or I'll bite you with my tooth! The mole is well-to-do and will make a fine husband."

The mole soon had four spiders working day and night spinning Thumbelina's wedding dress. The dress would soon be finished, and Thumbelina was worried that soon she'd have to marry the mole.

"Oh, I don't want to marry the mole. I want so much to be happy," thought Thumbelina. Just then she heard a noise. She looked out of the window and saw the swallow that she had revived.

"Oh, I'm so glad to see you," said Thumbelina. She hurried outside to meet the swallow and begged, "Please take me away. If I don't leave soon I'll have to marry the mole."

The swallow hopped down so that Thumbelina could climb on its back. As soon as she was aboard, it flapped its wings and flew high up into the sky.

Thumbelina looked down in wonder at the countryside passing below. She saw a large palace on the horizon, and to her amazement the swallow landed there.

"This is my home," said the swallow. "I think you'll be very happy here."

In the garden where the swallow lived, there were many lovely white flowers. Thumbelina reached out to touch the silky petals of the largest flower, and the flower opened to reveal a handsome little man.

He was no taller than Thumbelina, and he had a pair of beautiful, transparent wings on his shoulders and a crown on his head. He was the angel of the flowers. In every flower in this wondrous garden there lived such an angel, but this was the king of them all.

After the swallow introduced Thumbelina to the angel of the flowers, the angel said, "You should not be called Thumbelina. It is an ugly name, and you are beautiful. We will call you May, after the most beautiful month of the year." And with this she placed her hand in his, for she was happy at last.

And as May and the flower angel walked together through the garden, she looked overhead to see the beautiful swallow sailing over the horizon, singing its beautiful song.

THE UGLY DUCKLING

It was summertime in the countryside, and life was blooming everywhere. In this beautiful setting, a duck was sitting on her nest to hatch her ducklings. She had been sitting and sitting for a long time.

At last, one egg after another began to crack, and several little ducklings squeaked "Peep! peep!" One by one, the ducklings hatched and began to look all about.

"How big the world is!" said all the fuzzy yellow ducklings.

Then Mother Duck noticed that one egg hadn't hatched. *"The biggest egg is still there,"* she thought tiredly. So she settled down on the last egg until at last it broke.

"Peep! peep!" said the youngster as he rolled out of the shell. He was very big and ugly, and his feathers were gray.

Mother Duck looked at him and said, "You are a terribly big duckling. None of the others look like you. But you are who you are."

The next day was beautiful, and Mother Duck went to the lake with her ducklings. SPLASH! Into the water she jumped. "Quack! quack!" she called, and in the ducklings jumped, one after another. Soon they were all in the water, even the ugly gray youngster.

"Look how well he uses his legs and how he carries himself," thought Mother Duck. *"He's not so ugly when you look at him properly."*

"Come along with me and I will take you out into the world," called Mother Duck as she waded out of the water.

Soon they all came into the duck-yard. All of the other ducks looked at them and said, "Hmmf! Look at the ugly duckling! He doesn't belong here!" Right then a duck flew at the ugly duckling and bit him in the neck.

"Leave him alone," said Mother Duck. "He won't hurt anybody."

"He's too big, and so different from the others," said the duck who had bitten the duckling.

"All of your children are pretty, except that one," said another duck.

"He's not pretty, but he's good-natured," said Mother Duck, "and he swims beautifully." With that she stroked the duckling's downy coat with her beak.

As the family left the duck-yard, though, the poor duckling who looked so ugly was bitten, pushed, and jeered.

In this way the first day passed, but things only became worse. The poor duckling was chased by the other ducks. Even his own brothers and sisters treated him badly, and were always saying, "If only the cat would catch you, you ugly fright!"

Finally the ugly duckling became so sad that he ran away from home. He swam away when no one was looking, and spent the night in a quiet marsh.

The next morning two wild ducks flew up to him. "Who are you?" they asked. The duckling turned around and bowed to both of them.

"You are terribly ugly," said the wild ducks.

Just then a POP! POP! was heard, and the two wild ducks fell down dead right next to the ugly duckling. A group of hunters had arrived! The frightened duckling put his head under his wing. Suddenly, a terribly large dog bounded toward him.

The dog stood in front of him and snarled, showing his large, sharp teeth. After a moment, though, he bounded off.

"Thank Heavens," thought the duckling. *"I am so ugly that even the dog doesn't want to touch me."* The duckling lay still until the marsh was again quiet.

The little duckling spent a miserable winter in the marsh, hiding from everyone. He knew no one would like him because he was so ugly.

Eventually, spring came again. The sun sent forth its warm rays, and all of nature seemed happy and full of life, except the ugly duckling.

Deciding he would sneak out and get something to eat one morning, he flapped his wings. He noticed that they beat the air more strongly than before and carried him away rapidly, and before he knew it he found himself in a large garden.

Suddenly, out of a thicket came three beautiful white swans, floating gracefully by. The duckling was seized with sadness.

"I will fly over to these beautiful birds and they will kill me because I, who am so ugly, dare to approach them. But I don't care! It's better than to suffer the insults of all!"

He jumped into the water and swam toward the graceful swans.